Dear Hadley,

Soar High,
        Fly Far,
                See Deeply!

David Darst

Flim-Flam Flora

"Flim-flamming" involves
all the creative ways
a child devises to delay going to bed
and going to sleep.

Flim-Flam Flora

Written by David and Elizabeth Darst
Illustrated by Nicole Alesi

Illustrations by Nicole Alesi
Design by Claire MacMaster, barefoot art graphic design

ISBN 13: 978-0-9973920-2-9

Original "Tender Shepherd" lyrics by Carolyn Leigh,
Betty Comden, Adolph Green

Printed by Printworks Global Ltd., London & Hong Kong

First Edition

Wee Willie Winkie
Runs through the town,
Upstairs and downstairs
In his nightgown.
Rapping at the windows,
Crying through the lock,
"Are the children in their beds?
For now it's eight o'clock."

Meet Flim-Flam Flora!

Flora is a lively little girl
who greets every single day with

energy,

curiosity,

humor,

and joy!

All day long,
    Flora is busy with preschool,

playing with her toys,

going for walks,

and reading books with her parents
and her grandfather
(whom she calls "Daddy-O").

Meet Flim-Flam Flora's Parents

DAD

MOM

FAMILY

Flora's parents totally *adore* Flora and her younger brother …
every day Flora brings abundant magic, laughter,
and fun to her family.

(1 YEAR OLD)   (2 YEARS OLD)   (3 YEARS OLD)

Flora's Mommy and Daddy treat her
shenanigans, *tomfoolery*, and *rigmarole*
with respect and caring — for they know that
as *each day* seems to progress slowly,
each year is *flying by*!

Flora's Bedtime Routine

When it comes to bedtime,
Flora becomes a master flim-flam artist
(just like her mother was as a little girl)…

Flora's flim-flam routine
begins with choosing her PJs ...

"little bit too tight!"

"little bit too loose!"

"little bit too hot!"

"little bit too cold!"

Just like Goldilocks, that Flora!

Flora's Mommy and Daddy often take photographs
and videos of Flora's most successful flim-flams,
like picking out books to read at night.
Flim-Flam Flora's parents secretly love all of her flim-flam antics!

Flora pulls out book after book that she wants to read!
"Can we read *Heidi*?"
"How about *Cinderella*?"
"Can we read *The Surprise Doll*?"

This is a great flim-flam (one that her Mommy
used all the time too when she was a little girl),
because she knows her parents love nothing more
than reading with her!

Flora's Objects of Affection

Flora next needs to organize her stickers ...
her butterfly stickers, her bird stickers, her animal stickers,
her rainbow stickers, her sun stickers,
—*so many* kinds of stickers!

Flora calls for her dolls to join her in bed…
"May I please have Baby Maribelle?"
"How about Baby Fanny?"

Sometimes, the dolls are dolls in books…
"May I please have the doll with hair the color of butter?
How about the doll from France?"

Another good one is when Flora forgets a toy downstairs
—a ball, a flute, some blocks—
and she begs for that *specific* toy to be brought upstairs!

Flora's Questions

With Flora finally in her bed
she starts to ask where everyone is …

"Where's Daddy-O?"

"Where's Uncle D?"

"Where's Libby?"

"Where's Jessica?"

This is a great flim-flam because the list of people
is never-ending, and the answer is *always the same* …

"In bed!"

Flora wants to know where are her teachers,
friends, and classmates ...

"Where's Lindsay?"

"Where's Bella?"

"Where's Sam?"

"Where's Zach?"

"Where's Alexa?"

Flora starts rhyming and repeating the names ...
"Where's Ella and Bella?"
"Where's Jack and Zach?"
Flora laughs and laughs at all of this!

And then, Flora starts asking about the animals:

"Where's the Pig?"

"Where's the Sheep?"

"Where's the Giraffe?"

"Where's the Goat?"

"Where's the Monkey?"

Flora's mommy replies every single time…

"In bed!"

Flora's Blankets

"It's cold! May I please have a blanket?"
This is a great flim-flam
because Flora's Mommy
still brings out *her* baby blanket on occasion.

Flora asks nicely for *one blanket after another!*
Blankets,
blankets,
blankety-blank blankets!

Flora sometimes even asks for *Mommy's blanket*!

Flora's Sure-Fire Ways to Get Back Out of Bed!

Getting in bed for Flora does not always mean
she is finally in there *for good* …
Flora knows many ways to get right back out of bed!

One of her favorites is choosing her clothes for tomorrow.

Another one is to get down on the floor
and for *her* to read books to Mommy and Daddy!

Flora's Room

When she finally gets back in bed,
Flora wants to have just the right amount of light in her room …

(TOO BRIGHT!)

(TOO DARK!)

This is a great flim-flam because Flora's Mommy
was afraid of the dark too when she was a child!

After Flora's Mommy has gotten the overhead light just right,
Flora wants the bedroom door left open
so that *just the right amount of light*
shines in from the hallway!

Flora's Grand Finale

After Flora has selected her "just right" PJs,
    after she knows where her friends and animals are,
        after she has gotten the light just right,
            and after she has read her last "just one more book,"

it is FINALLY time for her Mommy to sing her prayers
and three rounds of "Tender Shepherd,"
    one fast, one slow, and one very, very fast …

As Flora's Mommy and Daddy
begin softly leaving the room,

Flora calls out, "Just one more hug?"
"Can we do a three-way hug?"

And as Flora's Mommy bends down close
to kiss Flora's head one last time and wish her a Good Night,
Flora softly whispers
"Just ONE more thing—can I tell you a secret? …

"I love you!"

Flim-Flam Flora is
finally,
finally,
FINALLY all flim-flammed out!

Tender Shepherd

Carolyn Leigh (adapted by Diane W. Darst)

Mark Charlap (arrangement by Yueun Kim)

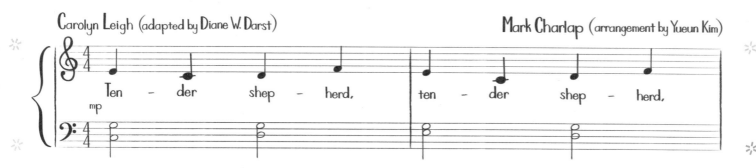

Ten - der shep - herd, ten - der shep - herd,

let - me help you go to sleep.

One, say your pray'rs, and two, close your eyes, and

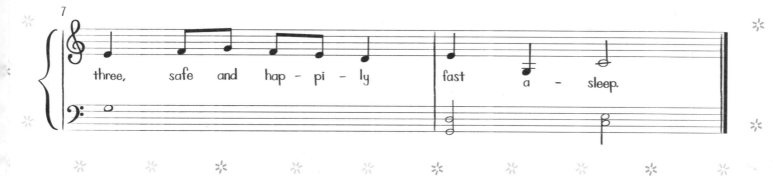

three, safe and hap - pi - ly fast a - sleep.